Milly and Molly

For my grandchildren

Thomas, Harry, Ella and Madeleine

Milly, Molly and Betelgeuse

Copyright © Milly Molly Books, 2003

Gill Pittar and Cris Morrell assert the moral right to
be recognized as the author and illustrator of this work.

Published by
Milly Molly Books
P O Box 539
Gisborne, New Zealand
email: books@millymolly.com

Printed by Rhythm Consolidated Berhad, Malaysia

ISBN: 1-86972-005-9

10   9   8   7   6   5   4   3   2   1

Milly, Molly
and
Betelgeuse

"We may look different
but we feel the same."

In a wild and grassy corner of the garden
lived an extended family of guinea pigs.

R Pit
Pittar, Gill.
Milly, Molly and Betelgeuse

Ma Guinea was mother, stepmother, auntie or special friend to all the little guinea pigs who lived there.

Ma Guinea knew all their names and stories
of where their names had come from.

4

Milly and Molly could lie on their tummies
all day long and watch the little guinea
pigs nibble grass.

But, best of all, they loved to watch
Ma Guinea gather the little guinea pigs
together for their bedtime stories.

Her quiet words filled the little guinea pigs with warmth and wonder and made them feel special.

She would begin... "Snowdrop. When the snowdrops push through the ground at the end of winter to gently herald the beginning of spring, the world rejoices. "Snowdrop," she said. "You are special."

"Popcorn. When a sprinkle of buttery, warm
corn jostles and pops and fills an entire
pot with softness and fluff, it's pure magic.
"Popcorn," she said. "You are special."

"Sweet pea. When the scent from a trellis
of soft pinks and purples fills the garden
to overflowing, it's the hot and dizzy
height of summer.
"Sweet pea," she said. "You are special."

"Chestnut. When the prickly case of the
horse chestnut splits, it bears a nut, more
smooth and shiny than a hand can resist.
"Chestnut," she said. "You are special."

"Bluebell. When we come around a corner
and feast our eyes on a carpet of blue,
the joy is in our exclamation.
"Bluebell," she said. "You are special."

"Pippin. When we crunch into a warm, freshly-picked apple, it is the taste and smell of pure sunshine.

"Pippin," she said. "You are special."

"Betelgeuse."

As always, Betelgeuse pretended to be asleep.
Ma Guinea didn't know where his name
came from, so she left him until last.

"Betelgeuse," she said. "You are special."

But Betelgeuse didn't feel special. He
wanted to know the story about his name.

Milly and Molly were sad to see Betelgeuse
so unhappy. And their extra attention
didn't make him feel any better. More than
anything, he wanted to know the story
about his name.

16

One night as Milly and Molly knelt
watching the stars, a particular little star
caught their attention. It waved and
twinkled and twinkled and waved.
It twinkled red and silver and gold.

Milly and Molly couldn't wait to tell Farmer
Hegarty about their friendly little star.

"That's Betelgeuse," crowed Farmer Hegarty with delight. "The friendliest little star in the night sky. Betelgeuse is special."

Milly and Molly were speechless.

They couldn't wait to tell Ma Guinea what
Farmer Hegarty had told them.

That night, after Ma Guinea had bedded
the little guinea pigs, she began...

22

"Betelgeuse. Among the millions upon millions of stars in the sky, there is only one little star that can wave and twinkle and twinkle and wave and catch your attention every time. Its name is Betelgeuse.

"Betelgeuse," she said. "You are special."

Betelgeuse was filled with warmth and
wonder. He felt special.

24

Milly, Molly and Betelgeuse

The value implicitly expressed in this story is 'building self-esteem in others'- making others feel good about themselves.

Milly and Molly help build Betelgeuse's self-esteem by finding the origin of his name. (Betelgeuse is the biggest, brightest star in the constellation Orion.)

"We may look different but we feel the same".

Milly Molly®

B O O K S

Other picture books in the Milly, Molly series include: